The Voice of Praise

Alvin Miranda

Illustrated by
Penny Weber

**WORSHIP MINISTRIES
INTERNATIONAL
WMI.WORLD**

The Voice of Praise
Copyright © 2025 by Alvin Miranda. All rights reserved.
No part of this publication may be reproduced, stored in a retrieval system or transmitted, in any form or by any means - electronic, mechanical, photocopying, recording or otherwise, without prior written permission from the publisher, except for the inclusion of brief quotations in a review.

Scripture quotations, unless marked otherwise, are from the Contemporary English Version, Copyright © 1991, 1992, 1995 by American Bible Society. Used by Permission Scripture quotations marked (NIV) are taken from The Holy Bible, New International Version® NIV® Copyright © 1973, 1978, 1984, 2011 by Biblica, Inc. Used with permission. All rights reserved worldwide.

Published by Worship Ministries International, Dallas, TX
English Hardback: ISBN: 979-8-218-83715-0
English Paperback: ISBN: 979-8-218-84251-2
Spanish Hardback: ISBN: 979-8-218-85732-5
Spanish Paperback: ISBN: 979-8-218-85733-2

wmi.world
First Printing December 2025
wmiemails@gmail.com

Publisher's Cataloging-in-Publication Data

Names: Miranda, Alvin, author. | Weber, Penny, illustrator.
Title: The voice of praise / Alvin Miranda; illustrated by Penny Weber.
Description: Dallas, TX: Worship Ministries International, 2025. | Summary: When a weekend with Grandma becomes a time of exploration and wonder, Daniel discovers that praising God is more than just singing.
English Identifiers: ISBN: 979-8-218-83715-0 | ISBN: 979-8-218-84251-2
Spanish Identifiers: ISBN: 979-8-218-85732-5 | ISBN: 979-8-218-85733-2
Subjects: LCSH God (Christianity)--Worship and love--Juvenile fiction. | Praise of God--Juvenile fiction. | Grandparents--Juvenile fiction. | Grandmothers--Juvenile fiction.| Family--Juvenile fiction.| Soccer--Juvenile fiction. | BISAC JUVENILE FICTION / Religious / Christian / Inspirational | JUVENILE FICTION / Sports & Recreation / Soccer | JUVENILE FICTION / Family / Grandparents
Classification: LCC PZ7.1 .M57 Vo 2025 | DDC [E]--dc23

To my grandchildren
Elijah, Ruby, Serena, and Violet
Thanking God for each of you
Precious gifts from my Heavenly Father
With all of my love,
Papa

Daniel loved playing soccer, and he was even happier when he sang to God. One day as his grandma made lunch, Daniel's voice filled the kitchen with his favorite praise song.

"Singing is a wonderful way we can praise God," Grandma said.

"What is praise?" Daniel asked.

"Praise can be telling God, 'Thank You for the birds that sing. Thank You for filling our hearts with songs that remind us of Your love. Thank You for these yummy tacos, our soccer team, and our strong legs to run fast,'" Grandma replied. "We can praise God all the time and everywhere—at home, at church, and even outside."

"There are many ways we can praise God," Grandma explained as she helped Daniel get ready for soccer.

The big game was filled with action from the start. With only a little time left, Daniel shouted to his teammates as they passed the ball back and forth. His heart pounded as he raced past the other team's players. With a burst of energy, Daniel kicked the ball hard. It zoomed across the field and flew into the net just as the whistle blew to end the game.

"GOAL! GOAL!" the crowd roared. Daniel leaped again and again, shouting for joy. "Yeah! We did it! We're the best! The champions! The greatest ever!"

Suddenly, something strange happened. When Daniel opened his mouth to speak, he couldn't make a sound.

He tried calling to his grandma, but nothing came out. Worried and frightened, he ran to her side and whispered, "Grandma, my voice is gone."

7

"Sweetie," she said, "when we shout with excitement, our voice can get tired and need time to rest, just like our legs can get tired after we run."

8

"Don't worry. Give your voice a chance to rest. You'll see.
It will be back before you know it."

10

"I know how much you love to sing to God. But remember, there are many ways we can praise God," Grandma reminded him. "Tomorrow at church, I'll show you."

11

The next morning, Daniel tried to speak, but still, no sound came out.

Inside the church, he heard everyone singing. It made him happy inside, and he wished he could sing too.

12

Seeing how much
Daniel wanted to sing,
Grandma smiled and said,
"There are many ways
we can praise God.
Let's see."

13

Grandma pointed to the front of the church. "Look at Pastor David! He's shouting, 'Hallelujah!' with so much joy as he he praises God.

See your Uncle John? He praises God by lifting his hands, and the man next to him praises by clapping his hands."

"There's your Aunt Mary. She's praising God by playing the piano, and the drummer is praising Him by hitting the drums and cymbals. The guitarist strums with joy, and the trumpet player lifts his instrument high as he praises. See the woman with the big smile? She's praising God by shaking the tambourine to the beat."

"And over there," Grandma smiled, "look at your friends dancing and twirling and celebrating! They're praising God with all their hearts."

16

"You can even raise a banner to praise Jesus for who He is. 'Prince of Peace' is one of the special names that describe Jesus. It reminds us He can give us a feeling of calm all the time."

Daniel never missed singing with his friends in the choir.
They took their places on the platform and began singing.
When he opened his mouth, only a whisper came out.
Daniel moved his lips to the song as his friends sang.

Grandma comforted Daniel as they walked home from church. "It's okay to feel sad about not being able to sing. Remember, there are other ways we can praise God."

Before Daniel went to sleep, Grandma prayed,
"Lord, You know how much Daniel loves to sing to You.
Please bring his voice back. In Jesus' name, Amen."

20

The next morning Daniel woke up to a special surprise. His voice was back! He jumped out of bed and ran to Grandma. "My voice is back! My voice is back! I can talk again!" Daniel shouted, laughing with joy.

"How wonderful!" Grandma smiled.
She prayed, "Thank You, Lord, for filling our home
with Daniel's voice again. In Jesus' name, Amen."
"What a perfect reason to praise God!" she said.

"Do you remember all the ways we can praise God?" Grandma asked Daniel.

"Yes!" he laughed with joy, thinking of each one.

"By shouting
'Hallelujah!', clapping,
lifting our hands,

playing musical
instruments, dancing,
twirling, and waving
banners."

"And," he paused, as a big smile
spread across his face, "by singing!"

"I CAN SING!"

Bible Truths About Praising God

Who do we praise?
I will praise you, my God and King,
and always honor your name.
Psalm 145:1

Why do we praise?
God loved the people of this world so much that he gave his
only Son, so that everyone who has faith in him will
have eternal life and never really die.
John 3:16

Who should praise?
Let every living creature praise the LORD.
Shout praises to the LORD!
Psalm 150:6

When do we praise?
I will always praise the LORD.
Psalm 34:1

Where do we praise?
Shout praises to the LORD! Praise God in his temple.
Praise him in heaven, his mighty fortress.
Psalm 150:1

I will praise you, Lord, for everyone to hear,
and I will sing hymns to you in every nation.
Psalm 57:9

Ways We Can Praise God

Singing
Sing praises to God our King.
Psalm 47:6

With musical instruments and dancing
Praise God with trumpets and all kinds of harps.
Praise him with tambourines and dancing,
with stringed instruments and woodwinds.
Praise God with cymbals, with clashing cymbals.
Psalm 150:3-5

Lifting our hands
Lift your hands in prayer toward his holy place and praise the Lord.
Psalm 134:2

Clapping our hands and shouting
All of you nations, clap your hands and shout joyful praises to God.
Psalm 47:1

Raising banners
Then you will win victories, and we will
celebrate, while raising our banners in the name of our God.
May the Lord answer all your prayers!
Psalm 20:5

Worship Ministries International (WMI) is a Christ-centered, Spirit-led ministry dedicated to teaching biblical and practical principles of praise and worship, with a focus on Spanish-speaking communities. The mission is expanding to reach children by sharing these same truths in ways that are creative, engaging, and easy to understand.

Alvin Miranda, founder and president of **WMI,** has over 30 years of pastoral ministry experience, teaching biblical and practical principles of praise and worship throughout the United States, Europe, and Latin America. He also serves as a college instructor and teaches piano to children. His passion is helping others pursue a lifestyle of worship. Alvin and his wife, JoAnn, are blessed with three children and four grandchildren.

Also Available from WMI

Lifestyle of Worship by Alvin Miranda is a 200-page study guide featuring 22 biblical and practical lessons on praise and worship from a non-musical perspective. It is ideal for pastors, church leaders, worship teams, and students. Available in English, Spanish, and Arabic.

La Voz de Alabanza by Alvin Miranda is the Spanish edition of the children's book *The Voice of Praise*. With soccer being the most beloved sport in Hispanic culture, Daniel's relatable story as a young soccer player resonates with children and families throughout the Spanish-speaking population worldwide.

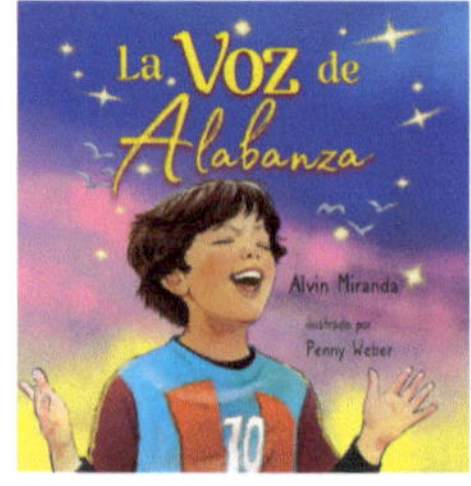

WMI.WORLD

For more information or to purchase books, go to WMI.world.